Story texts based on scripts written by
Carol Noble and Dave Ingham

Illustrations from the TV animation

produced by Tiger Aspect

PUFFIN BOOKS
Published by the Penguin Group: London, New York, Australia, Canada,
India, Ireland, New Zealand and South Africa

puffinbooks.com

First published 2007
Text and illustrations © Lauren Child/Tiger Aspect Productions Ltd, 2005, 2006, 2007
The Charlie and Lola logo is a trademark of Lauren Child
The moral right of the author/illustrator has been asserted
Made and printed in Italy

ISBN: 978-0-141-38367-5

characters created by
lauren child

My completely best ANNUAL 2008

This EXTREMELY **very** good book **belongs** to: *Abbey Russell*

I **live** at: *Scottland*

My **favourite** and BEST colour is: *PINK/PURPLE*

and this is a **picture** of ME...

(draw or stick your picture here)

PUFFIN

Contents

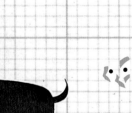

I have this little sister Lola.
She is small and very funny.
Lola is always very
extremely busy...

ALL about Us

(And our friends too!)

Lola loves **drawing** and **colouring** and **sticking**. Lola's favourite and **best** drink is **pink milk**.

Lola especially likes to **play** with her best, bestest friend Lotta...

Lola's best **imaginary** friend is Soren Lorensen.

No one else can see him except for Lola.

... Lotta and Lola like **giggling** and **dressing up** and **holding hands** a LOT.

They **especially** like to look after **Sizzles**, who is Marv's dog...

... Marv is my **best friend**.

Marv and me like playing
      football in the **park**
and doing things like
      finding out about **dinosaurs**.

We also have fun **making**

things like **rockets** that

can fly in outer space.

But **most** of all I like
      playing with my
little sister Lola.

Because she is small and
REALLY **very** funny!

5

WHO are you really most like?

(A funny quiz made up by Charlie)

Now that you've met some of our friends, you can play this quiz to find out who YOU are really most like! When you answer each question, write down the letter of your answer in the little box so that you can count them all up at the end.

You have been invited to a VERY funny **fancy dress** party. What do you dress as?

a)   a **monster**
b)   a **princess**
c)   an **alligator**
d)   a **vampire**
e)   it's a bit **tricky** to dress up when you've got **four legs**

What do you most like to do when you go to the park with your friends?

a)   play **monster** tag
b)   skipping
c)   collect **funny-shaped** leaves
d)   play football
e)   **chase butterflies**

What is your VERY **favourite** and **best book** to borrow from the library?

a)   **Animal World Records**
b)   Princesses and Fairytales
c)   **Beetles, Bugs and Butterflies**
d)   100 Things to Do with a Football
e)   any big book which is good for **snoozing** on

You have emptied your **piggy bank** and are going to the shops to buy yourself an **extra-special treat**. What would you buy?

a)   a big book of **dinosaur** facts
b)   **sparkly** hair bobbles
c)   some **extremely colourful** crayons
d)   a **comic book**
e)   a new sock to chew

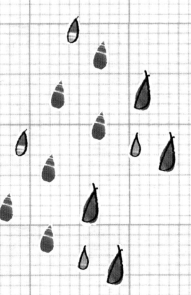

What do you mostly like to do when it is **raining** outside?

a)   build a **space rocket**
b)   dressing up
c)   do **drawing, doodling and sticking**
d)   make **paper aeroplanes**
e)   curl up and have a **snooze**

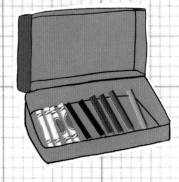

Now it's time to add up your answers!
      If you mostly picked the letter...

A	B	C	D	E
you are like **Charlie**	you are like **Lotta**	you are like **Lola** ✓	you are like **Marv**	you are like **Sizzles**

Choose the sticker of the character you are really most like from your special sticker sheet and stick it on the right space above.

Why not get your friends to do the **quiz** too!

7

A day in the **life** of Sizzles

(a **really** very clever and not at all stupid sausage dog)

Most of the time,
    Sizzles seems to do ordinary things like

eating, sleeping, woofing, walking, chasing birds and butterflies and then more sleeping.

But Lola and Lotta know
        that actually Sizzles is
        a VERY clever and funny dog.
They are completely sure that
        when no one else is looking
Sizzles can do absolutely
        ANYTHING like...

...juggling...

...and painting...

... and making cakes...

Lola says,
    "Sizzles really is a
    VERY clever dog."

And Lotta says, "Sizzles
        can do anything."

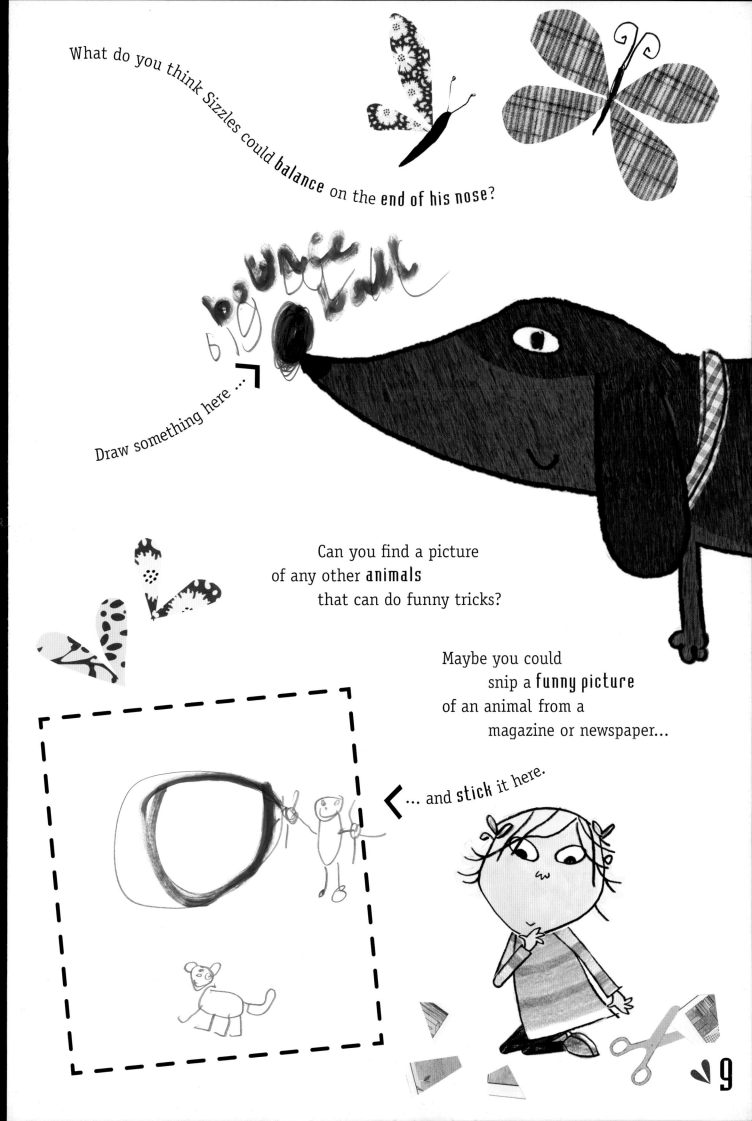

What do you think Sizzles could balance on the end of his nose?

Draw something here ...

Can you find a picture
of any other **animals**
that can do funny tricks?

Maybe you could
snip a **funny picture**
of an animal from a
magazine or newspaper...

... and **stick** it here.

9

I've won, NO I'VE WON, No I've won

(A very brilliant and good story)

I have this little sister Lola.
She is small and very funny.
        Sometimes we play "Who can sit still the longest!"
Lola always has to win.
        Last time we played, Lola said, "I've won!"
I say, "But I didn't even move!"
Lola says, "Yes... you did! I've won!
        I always win... always,
                always,
                        always!"

And then she says,

"I can beat a speedy, speedy cheetah in a running race,

and
I can drink my pink milk much faster than you."

I say,
"But do you have to win at everything, Lola?"

And Lola says,
"Yep. I've won!"

11

So I say,
"How about a game
of **spoons**?"
Because, you see,
I know I'm better
at the **spoon game**
than Lola.

But Lola says, "No you're not!"
And I say, "Yes I am."
And then Lola says,
"Ooh, Charlie,
what's that?"

I look up at the ceiling and then
when I look back at Lola...
her **spoon** has
definitely moved!
I say,
"Lola, have you... cheated?"
But Lola says,
"No, Charlie, **I've won!**"

12

So then I say,
"Lola, you remember how to play **snap**,
don't you?
You need two cards that look exactly
the same, then it's a **snap**."

Lola says,
" Yes, two cards that look
exactly the same,
then it's a **snap**."

So I say,

"Five."

"Ace!"

"Seven!"

"Nine!"

"King!"

"Queen!"

"**Snap!**"

So then I say,
"How about a game of **snakes and ladders**?
You go **up** the **ladders** and
down the **snakes!**

The one who gets to the **top** first is the **winner!**"

I roll first and I shout...
"**Six!** 1... 2... 3... 4... 5... 6...
and up the **ladder!**"

Then it's Lola's turn and she shouts...
"That's a three! **Snake!**"
I say,
"Lola, what are you doing?
Snakes are for sliding down.
It's the rules!"

Lola says,
"But Charlie, everyone knows **snakes** aren't all slippy and slidy.
They're easy to climb...
... I'm winning!"

Luckily I get another
six, which means up
a **ladder**!

But Lola says,

"AHA!
Dad said you are
not allowed to climb a **ladder**!
Not until you are
TWENTY-THREE!"

I say, "Uh-uh.

ladders
the   and
Up   **down**
                                                                the
                                    snakes.

That's the rules!"

So Lola
shakes the
dice and
says, "four!
1...
....2
.....3
.....4
snake!"

I say,
"Bad luck.
Now you've
got to slide
down
all
the
way
to
the
bottom.
I've won!"

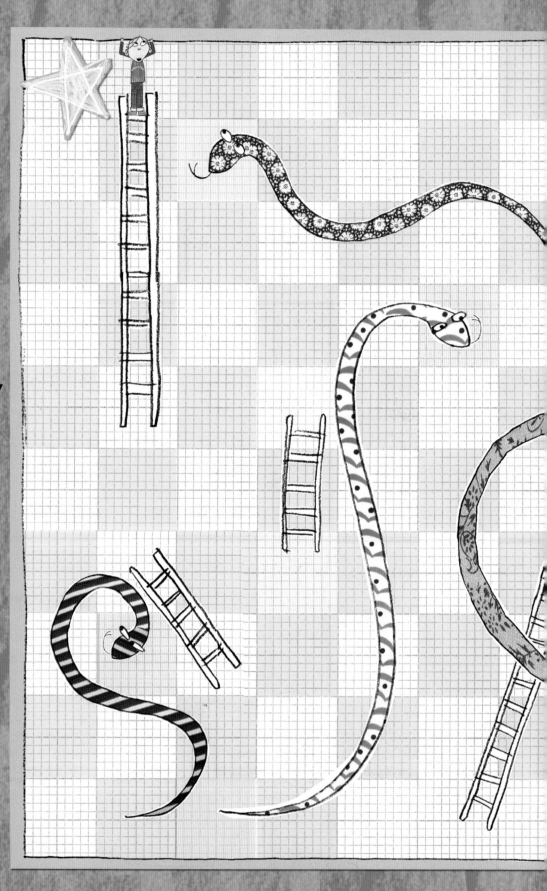

18

But guess what?
Then Lola pretends she's a **snake** charmer

and she charms the **snake** to the **finish**.

I say,
"But that's
cheating, Lola."

And she says,

"**No I've won!**"

So I think of something
that Lola could
    never, never **win**!

When we go to the park,
    I say,
"How about a **race**?
        It's **once** round
    the **bendy tree**!

Then **two** big swings
        on the **swing**!

Down the **slide**...

        and **first** one
to the **bench**
    is
        the
            winner! OK?"

Lola says,
"But I'm only little, Charlie.
I haven't been on the big slide yet."

And I say,
"Well, if you don't want
to win the race, Lola..."

Lola says,

"Steadygo!"

But of course I catch her up.

Then I say,

I say, "That's once round the **bendy tree!**"

"No you're not!"

And guess what? I'm actually winning!

"I'm winning!" says Lola.

"And two big swings on the swing!"

23

But then Lola calls,
"Charlie!
Can
you
help
me?"

And even though
I'm actually **winning**,
I say,
"All right, Lola,
I'm coming!
Hold on."

Lola says,

"Wheeee-eee!

We wh**oosh** down the slide together.

I'm winning!"

I say,

"Not
for
long!"

Then I say,
"And the
winner is...

me!

I've

won!

I've won!"

Then I remember Dad saying,
"Charlie, you must give Lola a chance,
because she's so small..."

And I say,
"Are you all right, Lola?"

And do you know what Lola says?
She says,
"That was fun!"

And I say,
"Even though
I won...?"

Lola says,
"Charlie, you don't
have to win
ALL THE TIME,
you know!"

At bedtime, I say,
"Are you **asleep** yet, Lola?"

And Lola says,
"Yes."

I say,
"How can you be **asleep**
if you are **talking** to me?"

She says,
"I'm
sleep
talking!"

So I say,
"The **first one** who falls **asleep** is the real **winner!**"
And then Lola whispers, "Charlie? **I've won!**"
And I say, "No... **I've won!**"
"I've won!"
"No... I've won!"
"I've won!"

Snakes
and
LADDERS

2–4 players

You will need:
Dice
Charlie, Lola, Lotta and Marv game counters

To **make** your own counters, choose the characters you want from the sticker sheet and stick them on to a piece of card. Ask a grown-up to help you carefully cut round the sticker shapes to make your counters.

How to play:
Choose which character you want to be and decide who is going to go **first**. Roll the dice and move your character the number of spaces shown. If you land on the bottom of a ladder, **climb** all the way up to the top.

If you land on a snake's head, **slide** all the way down to its tail. The first person to reach the gold star at the end is the **winner**.

I've won!

99   98

81   82

80   79   78

61   62

60   59

42   43

41

40

39

22

21

20   19

18

1   2   3

Start here

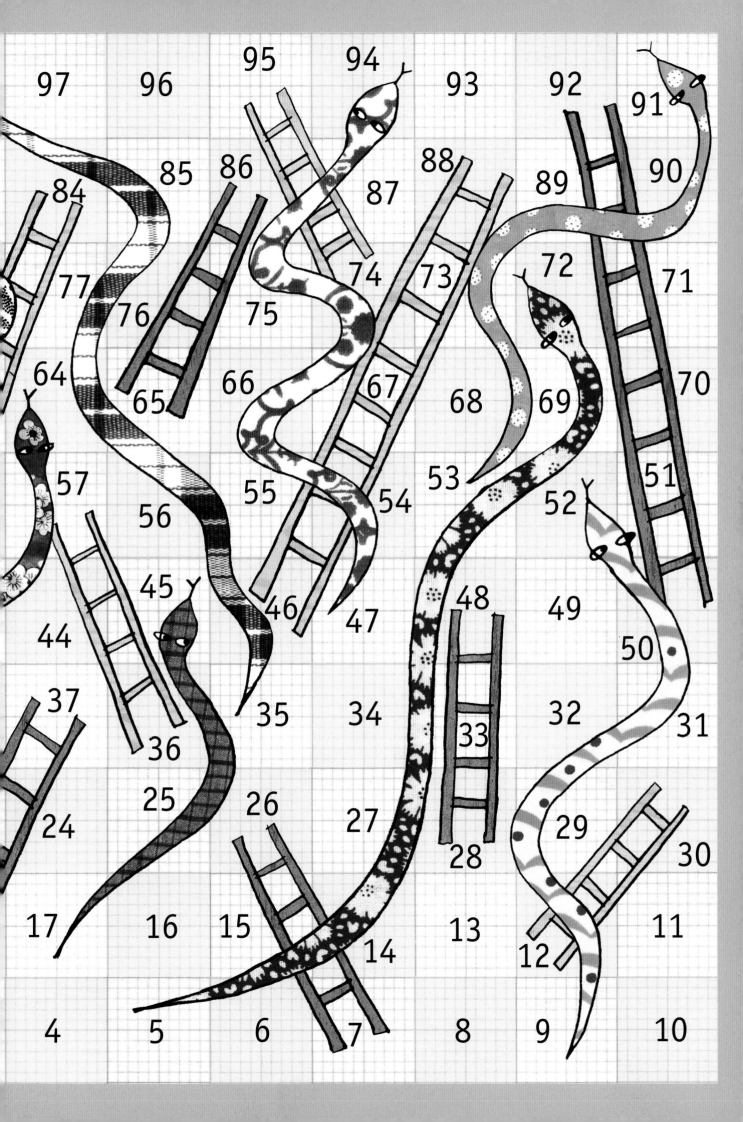

Charlie's page of AMAZING and REALLY very interesting animal facts

Lola and I have been looking at all the **animals** in my book of Amazing **Animal** Facts. There are some really VERY funny and interesting facts like:

Did you know that **cheetahs** can run really EXTREMELY fast? Sometimes they can run as fast as **sixty miles an hour** – that's nearly as fast as a **very** fast car!

Kangaroos are some of the bounciest animals in the world. They have very strong hind legs and can jump nearly as high as a **bus**!

"But I can jump even higher!"

And did you know that **flamingos** are all **white** and **grey** when they hatch. But they turn **pink** later because of what they eat. That's why some **flamingos** are more **pink** than others!

"I can be speedy too – look, Charlie!"

Whee!......"

"Ooh, maybe they've been drinking too much pink milk."

NOW let's see what YOU can do.

Try these little games with a friend. Don't forget to scribble down your results here!

Who can run the fastest?

Who can jump the highest?

How many times can you bounce like a kangaroo?

How long can you stand on one leg like a flamingo?

Indoory games for RAINY days

Lola's Funny Beetle Game

You will need: two or more players, dice, some paper and a pencil or crayon each.

Take it in turns to roll the dice. Each number on the dice means that the player can draw a different bit of their beetle. You need to start with a body, so you **absolutely** have to keep rolling until you get a **6** on the dice.

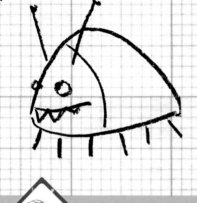

Here are the numbers you need to roll for each bit of your beetle:

6 for the body
5 for a feeler
(you will need two in total)
4 for a leg
(each beetle has six legs)
3 for each of the eyes
2 for the mouth
1 for some beetly teeth

The first person to complete their picture is the **winner**, and has to shout out **"Beetle!"** as loud as **extremely** possible.

Snap!

You will need: two players and a set of cards.

Have a look on the opposite page to find out how you can make your very own **special** set of **Snap!** cards.

Shuffle and deal the cards to all the players. Keep your cards in a pile, face down in front of you. One player at a time, turn over your top card and place it in the middle, making a new pile.

When a card is put down that matches the one on the top of the pile, it's a **snap**. If you shout "Snap!" first, pick up the pile of cards and put them face down under your cards. The game carries on with you turning over your top card and starting a new pile in the middle. Look out for any more **snaps**! The person left with all the cards is the **winner**.

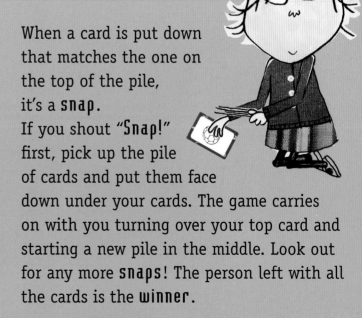

MAKE your own
Snap! cards

To make your very own set of **Snap! cards**,
snip out the next two pages from this book.

(Before you start snipping see page 36 for how to make a
special box to keep your cards in.)

You will need:
safety scissors (and a grown-up to help)
some glue
and some card
(an old cereal box would do)

Glue the pages on to some **card**, and then colour in
and cut round each one to make them into actual **cards**
that you can **play** with. Colour the backs of your **Snap! cards**
with a pattern to make them look EXTRA specially nice.

Make your own Snap! CARDS box

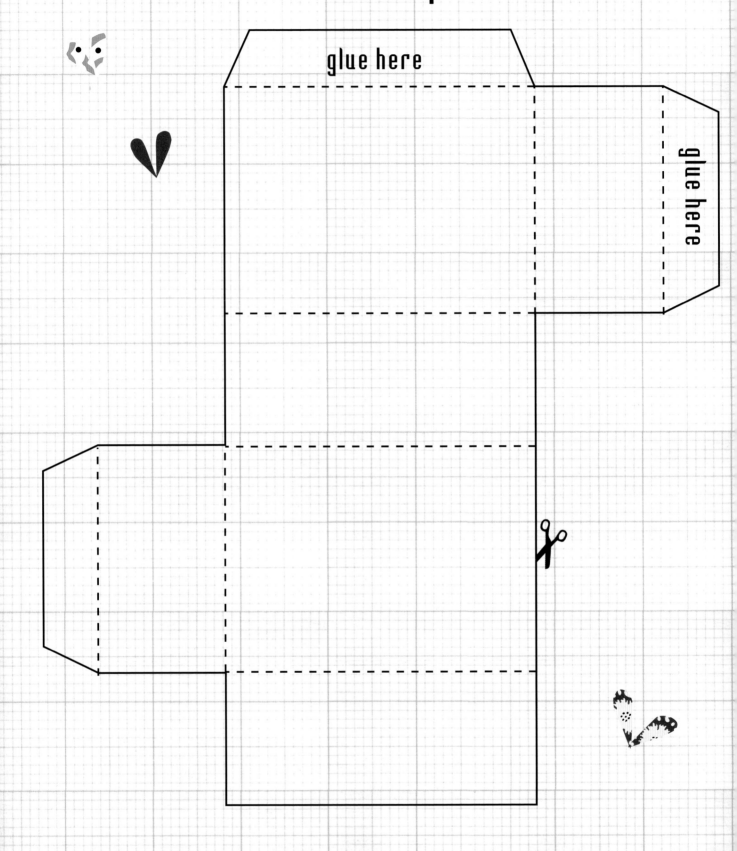

glue here

glue here

Copy this outline on to some tracing paper.
Then transfer the outline on to stiff paper
or card and cut it out to make
a special box for your Snap! cards.

Hopscotch

You will need:
one or more players,
a piece of chalk,
a surface you can draw on
and a pebble for throwing

Draw your hopscotch grid
and number each square
like in the picture.

The first player should throw the pebble on to square 1. Then everyone takes turns to hop and jump to the end, avoiding the square with the pebble.

Next, the pebble is thrown on to square 2, and everyone hops and jumps again. Keep throwing the pebble on to a new square. The first person to reach the last square without wobbling or falling over is the winner!

Monster Tag

. . . . "I'm a vampire! Catch me if you can!"

Marv is very good at playing Monster Tag! . . . .

Here's how to play:
One person is the scary **monster** and that person has to count to ten before trying to catch the other players. Everyone else runs away, and if they get caught they have to freeze until someone else crawls through their legs to release them. The game carries on until everyone is caught – or until the person who is the scary **monster** is really too tired to keep catching!

11

Do 10
star jumps
10

9

Have
another
go
8

7

6

5

Lucky you!
Have
another
go 36

Unlucky!
Back
to the
4 start!

7

3

2

START
HERE
1

Speedy race
around the
PARK game

This time you get to
make up your **OWN** game!

Use your favourite colouring pencils, crayons and stickers from the back of the book to decorate your game. There are stickers for extra tasks for your players or you could make up your own! You could have to sing a nursery rhyme, or spell your name backwards. You could even make your players do a **funny** impression of Sizzles!

How to play:

Choose which character you want to be (you can use the counters from the **Snakes** and **LADDERS** game). Then decide who is going to go **first**. Roll the dice and move your character the number of spaces shown. If you land on a square with a task, you have to do EXACTLY what it tells you – no cheating! Whoever gets to the end first is the **winner**.

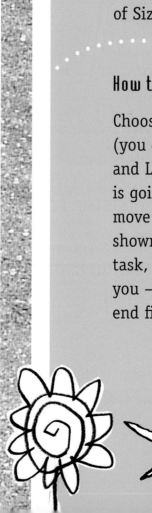

You WON'T like this Present as much as I DO

(An absolutely **good** and funny **story**)

I have this little sister Lola.
She is small and very funny.

Today it is Lotta's birthday. Lotta is Lola's best, bestest friend and Lola is going to buy her a present.

Lola says,
"Dad has given me some money
    to buy an especially special present for Lotta,
which she will like."

So I say,
"What are you going to choose?"

"I would like to get her an actual pony," says Lola.
"Because Lotta likes ponies."

I say,
"You don't have quite enough money to buy a real pony, but maybe you can get a pretend one."

Lola says,
"No, she would like a REAL actual one."

So I say,
"Lotta only has a really small garden.
So she couldn't keep a pony."

And Lola says,
"Yes, I can see that a pony would be a little bit squished."

41

So I say,
"A good present,
Lola, is one that Lotta can ACTUALLY use."

"Hmmm," says Lola,
"a REALLY nice
birthday present
AND
something useful...

A musical

skipping rope could be nice.

Or some
colouring crayons
that can colour
all
by
themselves.

Or some wings.
So Lotta can fly like a butterfly."

Then I say,
"Lola, another thing about presents
is that you need to choose
something that ACTUALLY exists.
All of the things you have just
said are made up..."

And Lola says,
"They're not made up, Charlie!"

"Yes, they are, Lola.

Anyway, Dad's taking us
to the toy shop..."

Lola says,
"I love the toy shop!"

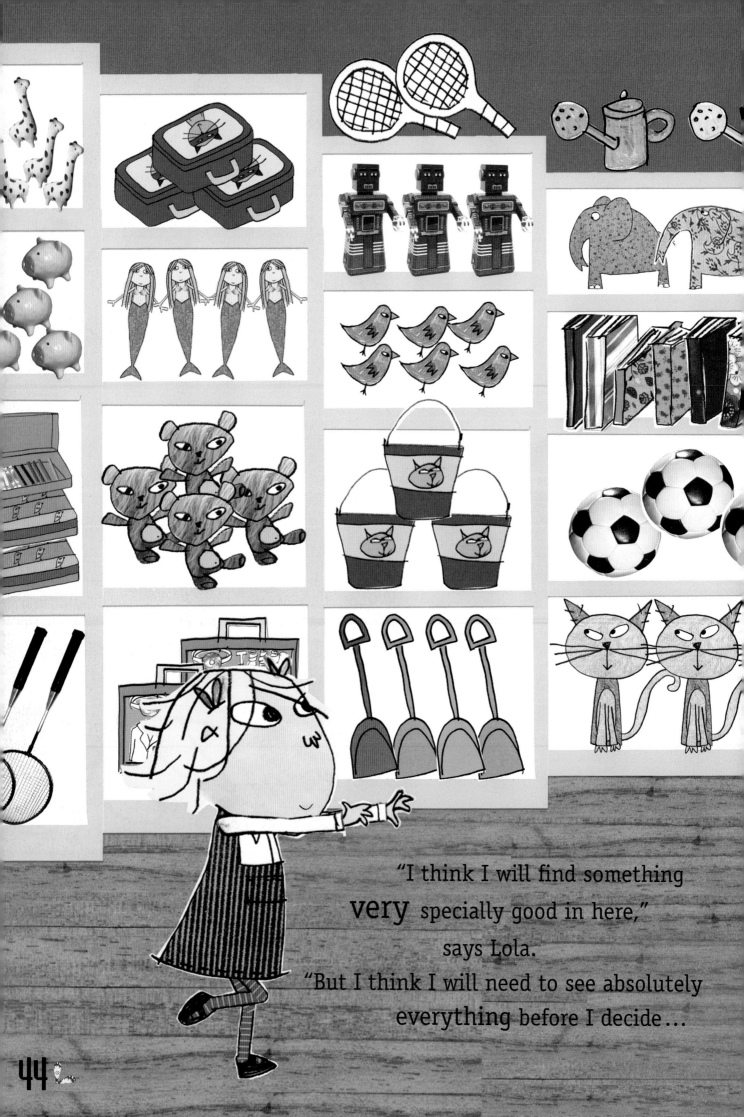

"I think I will find something
very specially good in here,"
says Lola.
"But I think I will need to see absolutely
everything before I decide...

LOOK, Charlie!
A Doctor Kit!
I have always REALLY
wanted a Doctor Kit..."

"But, Lola, we have come
to the toy shop to buy
Lotta a present... not you."

And Lola says,
"But that is all right, Charlie.
I can buy the Doctor Kit for
me and another present for Lotta,
because I have lots of coins.
One,
two,
three and
another
one."

"If you do that, Lola, there will only be a little bit of money left for Lotta's present. So you will have to get her something very, very small and hardly there."

Lola says, "Lotta will completely absolutely love this bouncy ball."

And I say, "But I thought you were going to buy Lotta a special present? It is her special day. If you love the Doctor Kit that much, I'm sure Lotta will love it too. She IS your best friend..."

"Don't worry, ill people, I am a doctor and I can make you better."

Lotta says, "So can I."

Lola says,
"Yes, she can. Because Lotta
is a doctor too."

So then Lola says,
"I am going to find Dad, Charlie,
and buy this Doctor Kit...

...for Lotta."

When we get home,
Lola is talking to her friend
Soren Lorensen.

Soren Lorensen is Lola's imaginary friend.
No one else can see him
except for Lola.

"That is a really good present, isn't it?"
says Soren Lorensen.
"I'd love to see all the bits."

"Maybe it will be all right for
you to have one little peek..."
says Lola.
"Just in case a VERY important
bit is missing?"

"Yes,"
says Soren Lorensen.
"That would be TERRIBLE,
wouldn't it, Lola?"

So Lola tears off a little!
piece of
wrapping paper.

"WHOOPS!" says Lola.
"I think now
we definitely
should open it..."

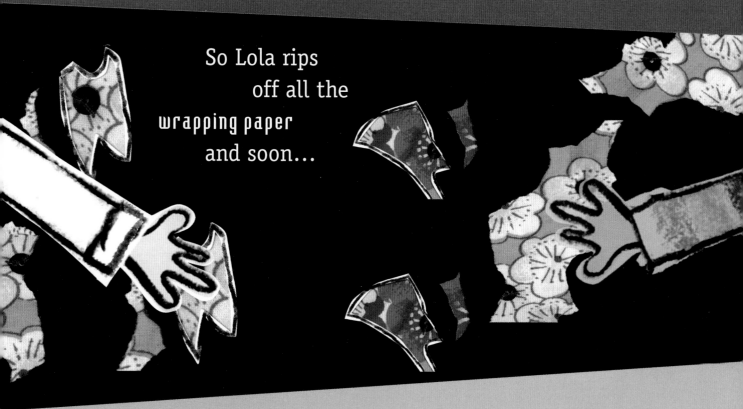

So Lola rips
off all the
wrapping paper
and soon...

... she is a **doctor**.

"I am a **doctor** and
I can make
you better,
Soren Lorensen!"

But then I go into the bedroom
and I see there are bits of wrapping paper
everywhere.

"Lola!
You've opened
Lotta's **present.**"

Lola says,
    "It was an accident, Charlie... we didn't mean to.
    Mmm... I was wondering,
maybe if I could keep the present
    and then I could give Lotta something of mine..."

So I say,
"But I thought you wanted
    to give Lotta something special.
She is your best friend, Lola,
        and you did buy the Doctor Kit for her."

"Mmm, OK,"
    says Lola.
"But will you help
me wrap it up again?
Soren Lorensen's
not very good at
    doing wrapping."

Then we go to
Lotta's house
for her
birthday party.

Lotta says,
"Hello, Lola... is that my present?"
"Well... er... it's..." says Lola.
And I say,
"Yes, Lola spent all day choosing it... didn't you, Lola?"

Lola says,
"Yes, I did. Happy Birthday, Lotta."

"Ooh!
A **Doctor Kit**! Lola!
That's what I really,
REALLY wanted.
THANK you!

Let's play **doctors** right **NOW**!"

"**Doctor** Lotta, is he still breathing?"
says Lola.

And Lotta says,
"Let me try the other knee,
Doctor Lola, because
his knees are
all
funny."

Then I whisper to Lola,
"Well, you chose a very good present for Lotta,
didn't you, Lola?"

And Lola says,
"I know.
I'm good at choosing!"

Lola's TOY SHOP shopping game

Lola COMPLETELY loves going to look at all the different toys in the **toy shop**. She has been saving ALL her coins to buy special **presents** for her friends. See if you can help her find what she needs. Look at the clue, then see if you can spot the right present on the **toy shop** shelves. Then help Lola by sticking each **present** on her **shopping list**.

Something **scary** to play a trick on Charlie!

A SPECIAL squeaky flying toy for **Sizzles**

Something for Marv to play with in the **park**

Something for Lotta's toy **farmyard**

An invisible **cuddly toy** for Soren Lorensen. (This one is VERY tricky to find!)

Lola has a few coins left over. What do you think she would buy for **herself**?

How to MAKE your own extremely VERY special pop-up cards

(for birthdays or any other special days!)

You will need:

Some strong paper or light card (if you can find it, cartridge paper works best)

Safety scissors

Crayons, coloured pencils or felt-tip pens

A grown-up to help you with the tricky bits!

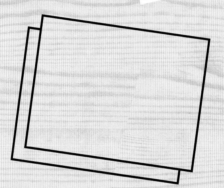

1 First choose two pieces of card that are **exactly** the same size.

2 Ask a grown-up to help you score one piece of card **exactly** down the middle. Then fold it in half.

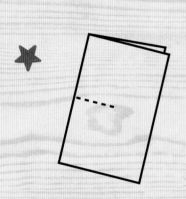

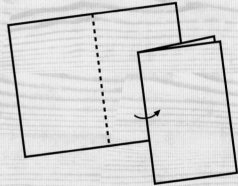

3 Next, use your ruler to find the halfway point along the fold and measure out a **straight** line. Draw it very lightly using pencil so that you can rub it out later.

4 Then you need to **draw** in a zig-zag line, along the nice straight line. Then **cut** along your zig-zag line.

5 Fold back the corners, away from the zig-zag line, then fold them **back** and straighten out the fold.

Everyone likes getting cards on their birthday.
Lola likes them so much that she even opened
MY birthday cards! My favourite card is
the SCARY MONSTER POP-UP CARD!
Here's how you can make one just like it.

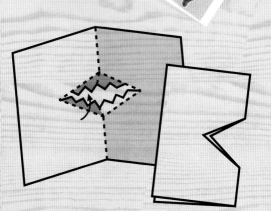

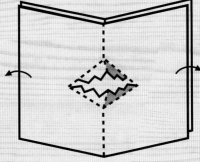

6 Open up your card and push the corners so that they fold **inwards**, then re-fold your card and press down firmly.

7 Now you should see a snapping, zig-zag **mouth**! Stick the second piece of card on to the back of your card to make the front and back of the card nice and **tidy**.

All you need to do now is draw the rest of your **monster** face. Don't forget to colour in the back of his mouth and maybe add a **slimy** tongue! You can decorate the front of your card too – maybe with crayons and glitter.

If you don't like **scary** monsters, you could cut the mouth in a **straight** line instead and make your mouth belong to someone else. How about a friendly frog or a bird or a smiley face? Don't forget to write a little message inside your card too!

Charlie's interesting FACTS all about BIRTHDAYS

People celebrate their birthdays
in different ways around the world…

In CHINA, some people put up **red** and **gold**
decorations to celebrate a special
occasion, as these are thought to be
extremely very **lucky** colours!

In RUSSIA, some
children don't have a birthday
cake, they have a completely
yummy birthday **pie** instead!

In GHANA, children sometimes have a
delicious treat on their
birthdays called "oto", made from
sweet potato.

And in MEXICO it's traditional to make
colourful papier-mâché piñatas in funny **animal** shapes,
filled with sweets and hung from the ceiling.
Everyone hits it with a stick until it breaks open,
then they share out the sweets!

All around the world, people have different ways of wishing each other a very Happy Birthday.

You might say...

Bon Anniversaire

in French

(Bon ah-nee-vair-sair)

С днем рождения

in Russian

(S-dnem-raj-den-iya)

誕生日おめでとうございます

in Japanese

(Tan-joh-bee om-eh-deh-toh goh-zai-mas)

... and

yadhtriB yppaH

(Happy Birthday backwards)
in Lola-language!

Do you know how to say **Happy Birthday** in any other languages?

My **birthday** is on:

20 Febuary

My best friend's **birthday** is on:

?

The **oldest** person I know is:

my Nan

The **youngest** person I know is:

Kara

Draw your birthday cake here!

Decorate it with as many candles as you will be blowing out on your next **birthday**.

fancy dress
PARTY
sticker fun!

Charlie and Lola are having a **fancy dress** party and have invited their friends to join them.

Use the stickers on your special sticker sheet to help everyone get dressed up.

Who wants to be a **vampire**?

Can you guess who might want to wear a **tutu**?

Don't forget that Sizzles needs a **costume** too!

Now that all the party guests are ready, it's time for some special party treats. Place stickers of your favourite food and drinks on the table – there might even be a little something for Sizzles to nibble on.

Lola says,
"That was fun, Charlie!
I **won** at completely EVERYTHING!"

I say, "No you didn't."

"Yes I did."
"Didn't."
"Did."
Then Lola says,
"OK, let's **play** the whole lot again!"

Use these stickers for the **snakes and ladders** game on pages 28–29

Use these stickers for the **quiz** on pages 6–7

These stickers are for **Lola's toy-shop shopping** game on pages 56–57

Hop 10 times on your left leg

If you talk before your next go, move back 3 spaces!

Move someone else back 4 spaces

Run round the room backwards

These stickers are for the **speedy race around the park** game on pages 38–39

Use these stickers for **fancy-dress party sticker fun** on pages 62–63